Bee Still

An Invitation to Meditation

by Frank J. Sileo, PhD
illustrated by Claire Keay

Magination Press • Washington, DC • American Psychological Association

Published by
MAGINATION PRESS®
American Psychological Association
750 First Street NE
Washington, DC 20002

Magination Press is a registered trademark of the American Psychological Association.

For more information about our books, including a complete catalog, please write to us, call 1-800-374-2721, or visit our website at www.apa.org/pubs/magination.

Book design by Gwen Grafft
Printed by Worzalla, Stevens Point, WI

Library of Congress Cataloging-in-Publication Data

Names: Sileo, Frank J., 1967– author. | Keay, Claire, illustrator.
Title: Bee still : an invitation to meditation / by Frank J. Sileo, PhD ;
    Illustrated by Claire Keay.
Description: Washington, DC : Magination Press, [2018] | "American
    Psychological Association." | Summary: Illustrations and rhyming text tell
    of Bentley, a bee from a busy, crowded, and noisy hive who teaches others
    to meditate in order to handle stress. Includes note for parents.
Identifiers: LCCN 2017036136| ISBN 9781433828706 (hardcover) |
    ISBN 1433828707 (hardcover)
Subjects: | CYAC: Stories in rhyme. | Meditation—Fiction. | Bees—Fiction.
Classification: LCC PZ8.3.S58254 Bee 2018 | DDC [E]—dc23 LC record
available at https://lccn.loc.gov/2017036136

Manufactured in the United States of America
10 9 8 7 6 5 4 3 2 1

Bentley is a lovable, calm honeybee.
He lives in a hive in a tall oak tree.

The hive is a busy and noisy place.
There is no wing-room; it is a crowded space.

The bees are always buzzing around.
A quiet place is nowhere to be found.

One day, the Queen told the bees to get busy.
This sent them scrambling into a tizzy.

"Buzz buzz! I'm late!" "Out of my way!" "Beg your pardon!"
The bees rushed out of the hive and into the garden.

But not Bentley. He chose to be patient and wait.
He decided to look for a place to meditate.

The honeycombs in the hive were just too tight.
Bentley thought of the garden and began to take flight.

He searched the garden for a place to be still.
When *bingo!* He spotted a bright daffodil.

Bentley landed on a petal and took a seat.
He closed his eyes and rested his feet.

While Bentley was meditating Bonnie Bee flew by.
She was gabbing with her friend Felicity Fly.

The two of them wondered what Bentley was doing.
They stopped to watch, their curiosity brewing.

"Psst!" they whispered to Holly Hummingbird.
The three of them giggled, "He looks kind of absurd!"

Soon a crowd had gathered on the ground and tree limb.
Bentley opened one eye and saw everyone staring at him.

Sammy Squirrel asked, "What are you doing, Bentley?"
"I am meditating to quiet my mind," he said gently.

"Sometimes I have too many thoughts in my head.
Meditation can help me stay focused instead."

"Working hard to make honey can cause stress for a bee.
But meditation creates a calm feeling in me.

Some emotions can sting, like anger and frustration.
I help soothe these feelings with meditation."

"Will it really help?" asked Carmen Chipmunk.
"I don't know, but I'll try it," said Sabrina Skunk.

"Can you teach us to meditate?" asked Billy Blue Jay.
They leaned in to hear what Bentley would say.

"Find a quiet spot to sit down. That's the first thing to do.
Your eyes can be closed or open—do what feels right for you."

"Next," said Bentley, "Take a breath in with comfortable ease.
Then let your breath out like a soft, gentle breeze."

"Notice your breath in your nose, belly, or chest.
Keep breathing slowly. Practice. Just do your best!

It's okay if a thought pops into your head.
If this happens, focus on your breathing instead."

Everyone took a seat on the ground or in the tree.
Soon they felt inner peace and tranquility.

A calmness spread throughout the garden and sky.
It began with meditation and a willingness to try.

Now, before the animals burrow, build, or pollinate,
they gather in the garden to sit and meditate.

So when life is hard or you just need to chill,
think of Bentley and try to *bee still*.

Note to Parents and Caregivers

Our lives appear to be moving faster than ever. We are in a constant state of information overload due to having a digital device constantly at our fingertips and access to around-the-clock news. We may have overbooked schedules, multiple commitments, and lack a healthy balance between work and downtime. It is common to feel overwhelmed, frustrated, tired, and stressed out. Similarly, children are exposed to many sources of stimulation throughout the day, including the computer, TV, and other electronic devices. They may also be involved in many social, academic, and extracurricular activities that keep them on the go and their minds constantly moving.

Children often mirror the adults in their lives as they learn how to regulate their emotions and balance work, rest, and play. And just like adults, they may benefit from turning off electronic devices and being present to what is happening to them in the moment. *Bee Still: An Invitation to Meditation* is a child-friendly introduction to meditation.

What Is Meditation?

Meditation is a practice for calming one's mind and body. Research has indicated that meditation can assist with improving concentration and focus, calming anxiety, and reducing impulsivity, among other benefits. Meditation takes time, commitment, and practice; it is not an exercise that should be applied only when your child is stressed out, worried, or lacking focus. There are three main types of meditation.

- **Mindfulness meditation** focuses on being in the present by bringing attention to the breath. By focusing on the breath, one may observe one's thoughts, sensations, and emotions and become more in tune with one's body and mind. Another focus during mindfulness meditation can be bringing attention to a bodily sensation or sound. Mindfulness meditation is the type of meditation Bentley practices and teaches in this story.

- **Mantra meditation** involves repeatedly focusing on a specific word or phrase, whether by repeating it silently in one's mind, saying it out loud, whispering it, or listening to it. *Om* is one of the most basic and common mantras people use. Using a mantra allows one to relax and focus on the word or phrase and avoid any distracting thoughts, memories, or sensations.

- Lastly, **guided meditation** involves listening to a trained practitioner or teacher in person or via a recorded media device. It may involve words, music, or both. There are many different types and purposes of guided meditation. Some guided meditations have a specific focus—for example, improving sleep. Others have a more general purpose, like calming the mind. Guided meditations often describe specific images or invite the listener to bring forth their own images.

There is no one best way to practice meditation. Not every method will appeal to your child. Try different ones and see what helps your child achieve the goals they are looking for. Once children find what helps them, incorporate it into their daily schedules and make it a regular practice.

Teaching Kids How to Meditate

This book was written to introduce meditation through storytelling. By reading about Bentley and the other animals practicing meditation, children may be more open and receptive to trying it themselves. The following are some tips for introducing and teaching meditation to children.

Create a meditation space.
Meditation should be done in a quiet place with no distractions. You can have your child sit on the floor, on a mat, or in a chair. You can purchase a *zafu*, which is a round or crescent-shaped cushion to sit on, or a *gomden*, which is a

firm, rectangular cushion that does not change shape when one sits on it. These cushions are not necessary, but kids may like them because they are colorful and it can become their "special meditation cushion."

Find a comfortable position.
When sitting, have your child sit upright with their back straight but not too tight. If your child complains they are uncomfortable, have them sit on a chair where the pressure is off their backs. Sitting down to meditate is usually recommended, but you can also lie down. However, people who lie down during meditating are more apt to fall asleep.

Make it a regular practice.
Meditation practice can be done at any time. Bedtime may be an optimal time to help your child unwind from a busy day and help them relax and assist with sleep. Whenever you decide to meditate, turn off all electronic devices to ensure no interruptions. Inform other family members that you will be meditating and that you do not wish to be disturbed. Although frequency is important for creating a regular practice, the experience should be enjoyable and not another chore in their already busy schedule. Never use it as a disciplinary tool.

Meditate together.
Meditation is an exercise that can be done as a whole family. When your child sees you practicing, it may make them curious to do the same thing. Share your experiences with your child. This will help them understand how meditation is applied in life. Teach them there are no right or wrong ways to meditate, and that over time with repeated practice, they will experience more results. Make the time together special and have fun!

Accept that thoughts might wander.
Our minds are constantly moving with thoughts randomly coming in and out. If this happens during meditation, don't worry! It is very natural for our minds to be busy. The goal of meditation is not to clear the mind completely. Let your child know it is okay to have thoughts and that their minds may wander. Let your child know that if a thought comes into their mind, to gently bring their attention to their breath. It is recommended that they acknowledge the thought but not get caught up in the story or details.

Start with short periods of time.
Sitting still in the beginning may seem like an eternity to a child. It can even feel that way for adults! Tell them it is fine to feel fidgety or sleepy. If your child is full of energy, it may not be the best time to begin practicing meditation. Start out meditating for short periods and gradually increase the time practicing. Depending on their age, three to five minutes is a realistic amount of time for children just starting out. Use a timer because it will indicate to your child when the meditation ends and keep them from saying, "When is this over?" Teach your child that with continued practice, they will be able to sit and meditate for longer periods.

Encourage your child.
Your child may feel self-conscious about meditation and respond by giving up or saying, "This is dumb!" Sometimes newness can create anxiety. Listen to and validate your child's feelings of uncertainty, self-consciousness, and not liking the practice. Validating your child's feelings may increase participation. Give children the opportunity to share their experiences as well! Do not to push children into meditation practice. This may increase resistance or anxiety about doing meditation. Encourage them to give it time. Applaud and reinforce their interest, effort, and openness. You can use reward systems for younger children; for example, you could say, "Let's meditate for a few minutes and then I will read you a story."

Vary the meditation practice.
There are many ways to meditate. In this book, Bentley practices mindfulness meditation

where the focus is on the breath. You may also try guided meditations or utilizing mantras (special words or phrases) that your child can reflect on while meditating. For example, they can meditate on the word "calm" or "peace," or on a phrase such as "I am relaxed" or "I am peaceful." You can also teach children to focus on things other than their breath, such as sounds, sensations, and smells. You can use objects to help with focusing. For example, watch a candle burn or put glitter in a jar of water, shake it up, and watch the glitter swirl around until it settles. Find the method that works best for your child and change it up to keep meditation interesting and fun. There are great meditation apps available for download as well. Some of them are free and some require monthly or yearly subscriptions. Search for what works for your child and for you!

Although meditation can be a wonderful, calming, and helpful practice for children, in no way should it be a substitute for professional help if your child is struggling with depression, anxiety, or other serious clinical issues. It is always important to consult with a mental health professional to discuss your concerns if your child is having emotional or behavioral issues that are affecting their social, academic, or other health functioning.

About the Author

Frank J. Sileo, PhD, is a New Jersey licensed psychologist and the founder and executive director of The Center for Psychological Enhancement in Ridgewood, New Jersey. He received his doctorate from Fordham University in New York City. Since 2010, he has been consistently recognized as one of New Jersey's top kids' doctors. He is the author of seven other children's books, including *Sally Sore Loser: A Story About Winning and Losing*, *Don't Put Yourself Down in Circus Town: A Story About Self-Confidence*, *A World of Pausabilities: An Exercise in Mindfulness*, and *Did You Hear?: A Story About Gossip*. His books have received gold medals from the prestigious Mom's Choice Awards and have won silver medals from the Moonbeam Children's Book Awards and the Independent Publisher Book Awards. Dr. Sileo teaches mindfulness to his patients, and to schools and organizations. He meditates daily and enjoys a cup of tea with honey made from honeybees every evening. Learn more about Dr. Sileo at drfranksileo.com.

About the Illustrator

Claire Keay lives in the South of England, where she works from her small studio at home illustrating children's books and stationery.

About Magination Press

Magination Press is an imprint of the American Psychological Association, the largest scientific and professional organization representing psychologists in the United States and the largest association of psychologists worldwide.